THIS IS FOR MOUTHWASH, SNAKES AND
LADDERS, ANYONE WEARING A SPECIAL HAT,
AND EVERYONE WHO'S AS DYSLEXIC AS I AM.

Silver Dolphin Books
An imprint of Printers Row Publishing Group
A division of Readerlink Distribution Services, LLC
10350 Barnes Canyon Road, Suite 100, San Diego, CA 92121
www.silverdolphinbooks.com

Printers Row Publishing Group is a division of Readerlink Distribution Services,
LLC.
Silver Dolphin Books is a registered trademark of Readerlink Distribution
Services, LLC.

All notations of errors or omissions should be addressed to Silver Dolphin Books,
Editorial Department, at the above address. All other correspondence (author in-
quiries, permissions) concerning the content of this book should be addressed to:
Oxford University Press
Great Clarendon Street
Oxford OX2 6DP
www.oup.com
www.oxfordowl.co.uk

ISBN 978-1-64517-002-0
Manufactured, printed, and assembled in Crawfordsville, Indiana, USA
LSC/05/19
23 22 21 20 19 1 2 3 4 5

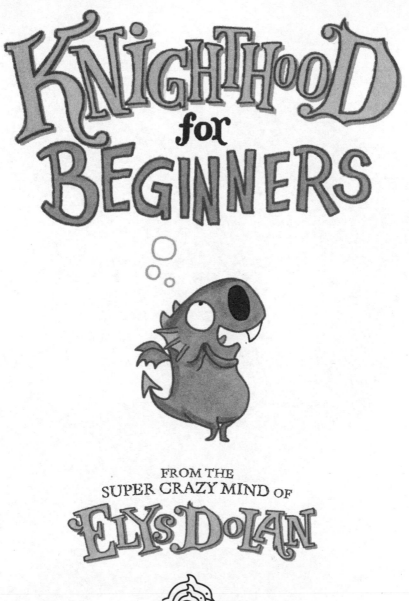

KNIGHTHOOD for BEGINNERS

FROM THE SUPER CRAZY MIND OF

ELYS DOLAN

Silver Dolphin

Prologue

There was once a dragon. A dragon called Dave. He lived high in the mountains surrounded by the bones of those who had dared to trespass near the dragons' caves. He was the most terrible of dragons, with scales, and teeth, and horns, and feet ...

. . . no, wait. Hang on a minute. I don't mean *that* kind of terrible. I mean he was terrible at being a dragon.

You see, all dragons must abide by Dragon Lore.

A dragon must hoard gold, gems, and all riches. He must manage it wisely and keep it tidy.

A dragon shall tell riddle after riddle with vigor!

A dragon must feast on nothing but villages.

A dragon must knit, because of all crafts, knitting is the fiercest..

To be honest, no one really understands about the knitting thing, but they do it anyway because that's the way it's always been.

Every dragon must master the Lore by the time they come of age and take their Dragon Test. When he's passed the test a young dragon will receive his certificate and become a fully licensed dragon.

No one has ever failed.
But Dave might be the first.

He'd been up all night studying, and first thing that morning Dave's parents came in and said they needed to have a "serious talk."

"Listen Dave," said his fearsome father. "As you know, you come from a very old dragon family. We're a proud line of the most dragony of dragons. There was your grandfather who had the biggest hoard since records began, Cousin Myrtle who once ate six villages in a row, and your Uncle Kevin who knitted that lovely hat."

"What we're trying to say," said Dave's massive green mother, "is that you've had the finest education, the best knitting tutor a gold hoard can buy, we've taken you to gourmet villages, and taught you our most cryptic riddles. We've tried our best to make sure you're ready, but your father and I both know you've never been the most talented dragon."

"You spend too much time reading those books and not enough time actually being a dragon!" said Father.

Dave has a thing about books. It all started when Dave was a baby and his parents went on a village-tasting tour. They left him with his Great Aunt Maud, who was a librarian.

(Even dragons need librarians.)

That's it Dave, you get your teeth stuck into enough books and there's nothing they can't solve.

It had a big effect on him.

And ever since then, Dave feels about books the way everyone else feels about their favorite teddy bear. If they're not a dragon.

Dave's father bent down and looked him in the eye. "When did you last set fire to anything?! Have you eaten a single village? And you never even finished knitting that pom-pom hat…"

Mother shot Father a stern look. "Now, Rupert, we said we were going to be calm about this. David, today is your Dragon Test and it's very important to us that you get your certificate."

"Get out there and eat a village, son," said Father.

"And don't forget your yarn!" said Mother.

"Assume your positions!" yelled the Dragon
Test examiner.

Yes, I did knit
this leotard
myself just
this
morning.

Dave looked at the other dragons. Maybe I don't have much experience, but I've read EVERY book there is, he thought. How bad can it be?

It turned out to be pretty terrible. Here are some snippets from Dave's report card:

Hoard Management: Dave was very well informed about hoard history but had not collected any gold of his own. Only treasure can be graded. FAIL.

And this was Arnold the Fearsome's Hoard from 1573 ...

Basic Knitting Skills: Dave's attempts were enthusiastic but ineffective. FAIL.

Riddling 101: Dave was unable to say his riddle due to stage fright. He was asked to get down before he had a little accident. FAIL.

Village Digestion: Dave did not manage to eat any of the village despite parental encouragement.

He commented that "it made him feel sicky." FAIL.

And so Dave became the first dragon ever to fail to get their Dragon Certificate. He was devastated and so were his parents.

Dave had never felt so ashamed. Or so hungry. (There is no dessert if you don't eat all your

village.) Dave knew an uncertified dragon cannot remain in the dragons' caves, and because he wouldn't be allowed to retake the test, he would have to leave the mountains forever.

Dave bid his parents a goodbye that was both teary and snotty in equal measure, and made his way down, over the bits of discarded armor and charred bones of people who had foolishly tried to climb the mountain to the dragons' caves. He was

just kicking away another helmet covered in tooth marks when he spotted something in the rubble.

It was a book.

15

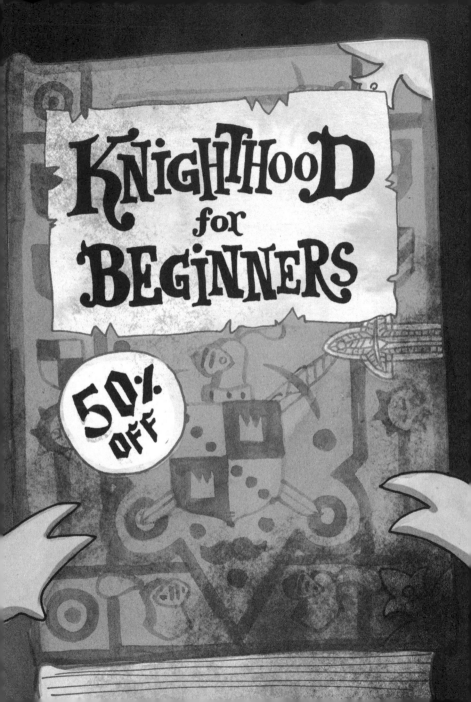

Dave read the introduction. It was a book about knights. Brave, helpful, kind knights who never had to do any knitting.

He suddenly knew what he should be doing with his life.

All he had to do was follow this easy-to-use, step-by-step guide.

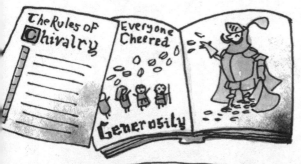

He sat down and began to read the first chapter…

Choosing your trusty Steed

CHAPTER 1

The first thing every Knight needs is a trusty steed. Select your steed based on physique, glossiness, attitude, and good looks. An eye for adventure is a bonus. Remember, the best Knights have the best steeds.

A steed! How do I get one of those? thought
Dave. Where do they live when they're not with
their knights? They probably hang out in fields
swapping stories of adventure, lifting weights, and
being fancy! I need to find one and convince it to
be MY steed.

Luckily for Dave, the kingdom had a booming
trade in used steeds, so it wasn't long before he
came across a field containing exactly what he
was looking for.

So many steeds! thought Dave. And I see
the perfect one. He's got all the things the
book recommends!

Dave was very excited to have already completed step one.

Dave jumped on his steed of choice.

BAAH!

"Wait! STOP!" yelled the steed, skidding to a halt. "How dare you! I am Albrecht! Adventurer, Explorer, Trendsetter, and Goat!"

Dave fell off with a bump, but he was too shocked even to care because THE STEED HAD SPOKEN!

Ja! I am a very rare talking animal.

remain still while I apply the frog...

ribbit?

bah!?

You see I had a run in with a wizard in my younger days...

"But we don't talk about the wizard thing! It's a painful memory. Now how come you can talk *mein kleiner grüner* friend, and why are you riding me?" said Albrecht.

"Everyone knows dragons can talk!" said Dave. "We also enjoy riddles, knitting, and occasionally eating villages, but I've not been much good at any of those. I chose you to be my trusty steed because you've got all the things the book said a steed should have. A physique, glossy coat, attitude, and good looks."

"I am very good looking and glossy," said Albrecht. "I was voted Miss Farmyard three years in a row. What is this book that describes me so well?"

Dave showed Albrecht the book. He studied it for some time and Dave was very impressed that not only could his steed talk, but he could read too. And admittedly he was very glossy.

"Knighthood eh? You're training to be a knight, *kleiner drache*? Why?" asked Albrecht.

"Yes! I'm terrible at being a dragon," said Dave. "So terrible that I'm the only dragon ever to fail the Dragon Test. If I become a knight I won't have to hoard gold, eat villages, or knit anything. I can be brave, helpful, kind, and have adventures!"

"ADVENTURE!" said Albrecht. "The finest of things! I do love adventure."

Once Albrecht had calmed down and stopped prancing, he had a think. "*Hmmmm*, I have been many things but never have I been a steed. You remind me of my younger self, *mein dorf esser*, and I think I can help you on your quest. Enough of the rural life! I will come out of retirement to be your mentor, trainer, life coach, and spirit guide! And trusty steed, of course."

To be honest Dave was finding this goat a tad confusing, but when you've found a steed this glossy you don't question it.

"I'm sure we'll be a great team," said Dave. "Now we should really follow the other steps in the book. Could you help me with number two?"

What's a spirit guide?

Aquiring the best Armor

A suit of armor is a must for any knight. The advantage of armor is that it provides protection from all things pointy, and is also conveniently wipe-clean. Make sure any armor can be easily removed in case you should need the bathroom on short notice. Armorers can usually be found in towns situated near

WHAM!
fig. 1

fig2
wipe!

castles. Find your bonus 10% off armor coupon in the back of this book!

"Aha!" said Albrecht. "I know where to get armor. We'll need to go to Castletown but we must be very careful, small dragon. I have a feeling this might be dangerous for you."

Chainmail Socks

no more stubbed toes

for low blows

CHAPTER 2

As Albrecht and Dave rode into town it became apparent that this was perhaps not the most welcoming of places.

"Okay!" said Dave, carefully tearing the coupon out of the back of the book. "I'm off to find the armorer. The book says I should tie you up next to a water trough while I'm away being knightly…"

"Halt, impetuous scaly one!" cried Albrecht. "Are you not looking?! This is not a place of dragon friendliness. Also, Albrecht does not drink from troughs. In my warlord days I used to drink from the skulls of my enemies! Now take cover *SCHNELL!*"

It's a smoothie. I'm on a detox.

In a place of safety, Albrecht and Dave discussed their next move.

"I know we dragons have a bad reputation but surely this is overdoing it," said Dave.

10% off!

"Perhaps the armorer is a more friendly sort of person? If I explain my quest nicely I'm sure he'll help."

"No Dave," said Albrecht. "I do not think he would help."

"But this is a disaster!" said Dave. "The book says I must have armor if I'm going to be a knight. And I don't think I'm a standard size, I'll need custom-made armor! Oh, and the coupon... it's just such a good deal."

"Do not worry scaly one," said Albrecht. "I know how to get you some *kleine* Dave armor. You stay out of sight and Albrecht will take care of it..."

Town Armorer

DRAGON"S BANE

DRAGON POKER

DRAGON SLICER

DRAGON CRUSHER

Albrecht knew the mighty battle ahead would require all of his skills. It began with a contest of strength and determination…

…then of style and grace…

...and finally, a battle of wits and cunning.

At last Albrecht emerged victorious!

Back outside the tavern, Dave was thrilled with his nearly-new suit of armor.

Just as Dave got his moustache on straight, he found himself covered by a huge shadow. It belonged to a knight. A big knight. Actually, a really massive knight.

"He must have eaten an entire village on his own to get that big!' said Dave.

"*Pff,* he's not that big," said Albrecht. "I once knew a whale that was twice the size of him…"

"We didn't steal any armor. My name is Dave, and this is my trusty steed Albrecht, and I'm trying to become a knight…"

"A KNIGHT!' cried Gnasty. "A tiny, little, green man like you! HA! That's the most ridiculous thing I've ever heard. As the King's Chief Knight and enforcer, I'm arresting you both for armor theft, being weirdly green, and smelling kind of goaty."

"Dave does not smell goaty!" Albrecht yelled as they were marched off.

"Don't worry," said Dave. "I've still got the book."

I'm actually starting to enjoy the breeze around my pants.

Do you know who I am?!

CHAPTER 3

"Get in there, thieves!" shouted Sir Gnasty as he flung Dave and Albrecht into the disturbingly slimy castle dungeon.

"But really we didn't steal the armor!" said Dave. "We won it."

"It was a regulation game of snakes and ladders!" added Albrecht.

"Knights just don't steal," said Dave.

"Stop with this knight talk!" said Gnasty. "Anyway, I must be off to plot against the King, I mean, er, have lunch."

And he slammed the door and stomped off down the passage.

"That knight is *ÜBER* awful but it could be worse," said Albrecht. "I was once imprisoned in the tallest of towers. I had to grow my hair so long and convince a prince I was marriage material. Crazy times!"

"That's . . . interesting," said Dave. "There must be something in the book about escaping from dungeons."

Dave pulled the book from its hiding place and started flipping through its pages. "Yes! Look here. There are even diagrams! I love diagrams."

Escaping Unfair Imprisonment

During a quest it is not uncommon for even the most experienced knight to become entangled in some misunderstanding resulting in unfair imprisonment. Reasons for imprisonment can include:

- Capture by enemy
- Mistaken identity
- Offending kings

- Parking violations
- Flashy dressing
- Bad dancing
- Picking your nose and eating it

In the case of no conveniently-sleeping jailers or easily-discovered secret passages there's a simple solution. Use your Knightly strength! See diagram below:

Fig.1   Fig.2   BAM!

Huzzah!

Dave hauled himself up and fixed his gaze on the door. "Okay, I'm going to do this. I'm going to use my knightly strength!"

"*Meine* Dave," said Albrecht, "that door is very big and solid and you are so small and green . . ."

But Dave had already stepped back . . . he focused... then he ran like the wind . . . and gave a mighty leap . . . !

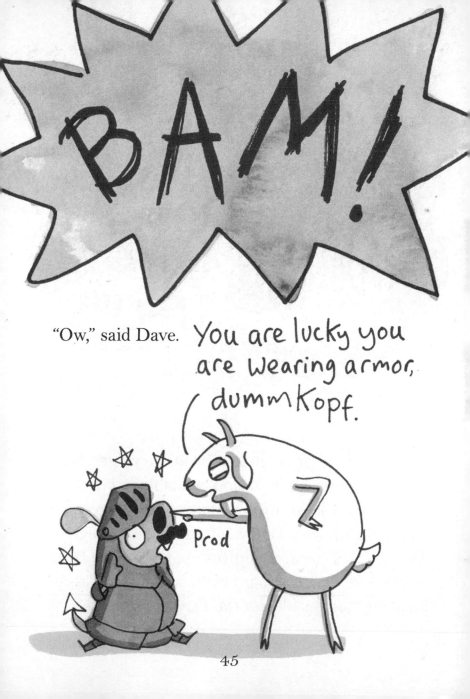

"Ow," said Dave. You are lucky you are wearing armor, dummkopf.

Prod

Before Dave could see straight again, the door creaked open and in walked the jailer with their evening meal.

"Good evening prisoners," said the jailer. "We have a wide selection of slop available today. There's the Classic Brown slop, always a favourite. The 1542 Chunky Yellow, an excellent vintage. The XXX Super Hot Chilli slop, not for the faint-hearted. If you're feeling brave, we have Mystery Slop, and today's Slop of the Day is: Green."

"I'll take a bowl of the 1542 Yellow and a XXX Super Hot for my fiery friend," said Albrecht.

"Very good, sir. Welcome to the dungeons and I hope you enjoy your stay," said the jailer, locking the door behind him.

"But we don't need slop!" said Dave. "We need to escape!"

"If life has taught me anything it's never say no to a free bowl of slop," said Albrecht, enthusiastically eating the chunks out of his Yellow. He handed the other bowl to Dave.

"I'm never going to be a knight if I'm stuck in here!" Dave flung his bowl across the room. It smashed onto the ground with an appropriate SLOP! noise and Dave went to sulk in the corner.

Albrecht was only halfway through his slop (he still wasn't 100% sure what the chunks were, but they had a not unpleasant fish/socks/breath mint flavor to them) when he heard a sizzling sound coming from the floor.

He turned to look. "Dave my *kleine suppe werfer*! With your XXX Super Hot Chilli slop, I think you found our way out. GENIUS!"

Would Sirs care for some
dessert slop...
Darn! This keeps happening.

CHAPTER 4

In another part of the castle, Sir Gnasty had chosen the King's bathtime as the perfect moment to launch his evil plan.

Huge sack? Check!... Net? Check!... Rope? Check! Excellent.

Now we're totally ready to complete my evil plan to kidnap the king and make the kingdom mine! With me, Army of Evil!

Just as Dave and Albrecht slid their way up a drainpipe and out into the light, Gnasty and his Army of Evil crashed through the King's bathroom door.

Everyone looked a little shocked.

Oh! Hello there! This is weird isn't it?

THE THRONE

"How did they get in here?!" asked Gnasty. "We can't possibly stage this kidnapping in front of witnesses . . . ! Erm, I mean, your Majesty! I was just waiting to be of assistance and definitely not plotting your downfall. Let me deal with those prisoners."

Albrecht shook toilet water off his now not-so-glossy coat and addressed the King with an overly fussy bow. "Your Majesty, I must throw myself upon your mercy! I am but a simple goat/steed/life coach accompanying young Dave on his quest to become a knight..."

"Sire, they are thieves!" Gnasty butted in.

"I won that armor fair and square!" shouted Albrecht getting angry. "Sir Ironpants is a terrible snakes and ladders player!"

How dare you insult my Snakes & ladders skills! This means fisticuffs!

He's not worth it Albrecht!

"Wait!" said Dave. "Your Kingness, Sir! If I could just have a word? My dream is to be a knight. I've been reading a lot about them and knights are good, kind, and honest so I wouldn't ever steal! Is there some way I can prove myself?"

"*Hmmm,*" the King considered. "I like the way you toilet chaps work. I'm impressed by your daring, if stinky, escape from my dungeons, and I admire your pale green complexion."

I tell you what... TRIAL BY COMBAT!

You can fight for the right to be a knight!) Don't stand up Sire!

"If you can beat all my knights in single combat then I will make you a knight, Dave my boy. Tomorrow I will hold a tournament!"

"Is that a thing?" Albrecht asked Dave.

Dave gasped. "Yep, look here, under 'special circumstances.' If you win a tournament, the King has the power to grant an instant knighthood."

Tournaments, single combat, and hitting with swords.

For a tournament you will need

A fancy tent
To hang around in before and after fighting.

your steed
looking their most glossy.

Many Weapons

CHAPTER 5

Early the next morning, Dave was already up and studying hard. "I've been reading about tournaments and single combat and hitting people with swords. There's so much to learn. Just look at all this…"

Turn the page for some

Handy Hints and Tips

"And that's just one page!" said Dave.

Albrecht snatched the book away. "Dave, as your trusty steed I am confiscating this book! We do not have to do things the *dummkopf* knight way. We shall solve this using our GENIUS, not ridiculous hitting."

Dave was about to protest, but it was time to head out to the jousting field.

Waiting for the tournament to begin, Dave was feeling incredibly nervous without the book. "But Albrecht, we're not knights, we don't know how to win a tournament! If I could just check a few things about hitting with swords…"

"Worry not, scaly one," said Albrecht. "Everyone has a weakness. Let's study our opponents and see what we can learn."

No worries Klein Dave, Albrecht knows what to do.

PROD

These knights don't seem much like the ones in the book, thought Dave, as he watched Sir Ironpants do another set of disturbing lunges. So they went to have a look at the other knights.

"See *meine* Dave, *dummköpfe*!" whispered Albrecht. "I have a plan for nearly all of them…"

Just then, he was interrupted by the sound of trumpets.

First came Sir Ironpants, who was very ticklish without his armor.

Then Sir Snoz, who had terrible hay fever.

Sir Mightybrow was nothing without his glasses.

Sir Butterball had a big soft spot for his pie.

The mighty lungs of Dame Hilda were almost too much for Dave and Albrecht.

But Albrecht found another use for Butterball's pie.

Thrilled with their victories, Dave could almost smell the knighthood.

"This is going rather well," said Dave.

REAL KNIGHTS JOUST!

CHAPTER 6

With just one knight left to vanquish Albrecht explained his plan for Sir Gnasty. It would involve beards, mice, and hair spray, but Gnasty had a surprise for them.

Albrecht looked perturbed. "I had a plan to defeat one huge Gnasty, but a huge Gnasty, on a massive horse, with a super long, pointy stick? I can see no weakness here!"

Dave went pale and felt like he needed the bathroom.

But wait… if he was a real knight he wouldn't just go to the bathroom. He'd fight Gnasty with his big horse and his big stick anyway. It was time to use some of that bravery the book talked about.

"Okay, Albrecht, I remember something about having to "stay on your steed no matter what" so I'll hang onto you with everything I've got and we'll figure out some way to knock Gnasty off his horse."

When the joust began, Albrecht and Dave weren't doing so well.

But Dave refused to let go of Albrecht, even when Gnasty gave them such a whack with his lance that they flew straight up into the air. Gleeful, Gnasty listened to the crowd's applause and waited for his opponents to hit the ground so he could give them an even bigger whack.

But they didn't come down.

Gnasty looked puzzled for a moment then broke into a huge grin. "I jousted them so hard I smashed them into oblivion! I'm so talented, so amazing, so STRONG! Look at my quads!"

QUADS!

As Gnasty flexed his muscles for the crowd, Dave and Albrecht were having a hasty conversation above him.

"I can't hang on for long!" said Dave.

"Eugh, if you let go we'll hit the ground and that *dummkopf* will whack us again!" said Albrecht, wriggling.

Dave's eyes widened as he thought of a brilliant idea. "But maybe we don't have to hit the ground! Brace yourself, I'm letting go."

How much do you weigh!?

Your feet are so pointy!

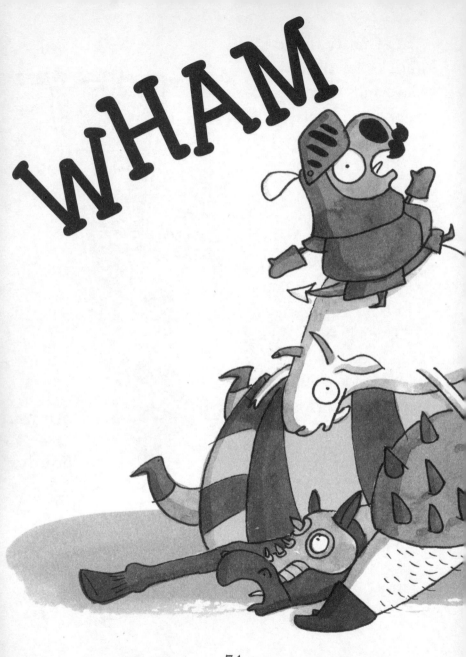

"Oh, now look at that.
Dave is the WINNER!"
declared the King.
    And the peasants went wild.

Dave scrambled down from the heap, but before he could check on Albrecht, Gnasty hauled himself up and bawled at the King. "THEY WERE OBVIOUSLY CHEATING! That's not how you knock a knight off his steed!"

"And he gave away my pie!" Sir Butterball joined in. "That's just not right."

Soon all the knights were accusing Dave of cheating.

"SILENCE!" said the King. "All right then, we'll settle this once and for all. I hear there's a peasant uprising in town. They're nothing but trouble, those peasants. Gnasty, you and Dave will go down there and the first one to stop the rioting will be the winner and I'll make them Chief Knight!"

"That sounds *wunderbar*," said Albrecht. "And I also may need medical attention…"

CHAPTER 7

As they rounded a corner to see the Dragon's Head tavern, things didn't look great.

Dave flinched. "Oh dear me, there's some dirty fighting going on here."

"Dirty? Ha!" said Albrecht. "When I was a professional mud wrestler we did the dirty fighting. This is all squeaky clean."

BELLY SLAM!

Gnasty came barreling down the hill behind them and ran straight into the crowds of flailing peasants. "You want a riot do you?!" he shouted.

"I'll punch the riot right out of you all!"

"We have to do something fast before someone really gets hurt," Dave said, getting concerned. "I'll just take a really quick look at the book."

easants and their habits

Peasants are smelly ..

Weird ..

and obsessed with rat-on-a-stick.

They are constantly fighting with each other and there's only one way to solve it.

Talk with your Fists!

Dave may have read the page a little too quickly. "Right, it… um… says something about talking to them. That seems sensible. I'll go over there and have a chat with that man hitting that other man with a chicken."

Albrecht thought this would probably lead to Dave also getting hit with a chicken, but Dave was already chatting.

"Hello, Mr. Peasant Sir, what seems to be the problem?" asked Dave.

The peasant, known in the town as Boil Man mainly because of his boils, was so shocked at being spoken to nicely by a knight that he dropped his chicken.

"Well… err…we're dissatisfied with our health-care system!" Boil Man told him. "The doctor is terrible!"

"The only thing we can do is BRAWL!" added Carbuncle Guy, happy that he was no longer being hit by a chicken.

"This does not bode well for *meine hintern*," said Albrecht. "How bad is this doctor?"

Boil Man explained.

Well it's like this you see...

I have a paper cut.
Lick this sheep at sunset for 5 days.

Bah?

"*Pah*, I'd make a better doctor than him!" said a large woman with a large beard (that's right, beard), startling Boil Man and Carbuncle Guy so much they scurried off back into the brawl.

"Would you?" asked Dave.

"Well, yes, actually. Watch this."

"My hintern hasn't been in such trouble since the cannibalistic Sheep Men of Bahbahland ate my tail! I have a wooden one now . . . but how did you learn medicine, hairy lady?"

And so the Bearded Lady began to explain.

Ever since she was a girl the Bearded Lady had been forced to earn her living by sitting in her stall and charging people to stare at, tug on, or

run screaming from her beard. Her stall bordered the first aid, counseling, and aromatherapy sections of the bookstall next door. She used to read the stock while the people pointed and screamed. Gradually she picked up a wide range of medical skills. There was one book on fly-fishing in there, so she's not too bad at that, either.

"I wish I could open a clinic," she said, "but who would want to be treated by a bearded lady?"

"You could shave?" suggested Albrecht.

The Bearded Lady looked furious. "I came to terms with the fact that I'm a bearded lady years ago and I won't change just because people are narrow-minded. Plus, this is the most beautiful beard in the whole kingdom. It's a work of art!"

"Maybe you could team up with the doctor?" said Dave. "Let's go and talk to him."

"Don't forget about the task, Dave!" said Albrecht. "Who would not want to help this lovely hairy lady, but we can't let Gnasty win."

"But if we can solve this doctor problem we can stop the riot." said Dave. "What have we got to lose?"

CLOSED

CHAPTER 8

DOCTOR

No boils   No plague   No teeth

NO Time wasters!

REASONABLE RATES

50% OFF leech treatments

Dave peeked round the door and said, "It doesn't look like there's anyone home."

"*Hmm,* you are correct Dave. Is he in the back having a tea break maybe?"Albrecht went over to a curtain covering a door at the back of the room and pulled it open. "*MEINE GOTT*! What is this?!"

"DON'T LOOK AT ME!" shouted the doctor. "I'm so ashamed!"

"It's just that I've always wanted to be a fool. The glamour, the applause, the hat, the bells! I made my own costume and I can nearly do a headstand. Don't tell my patients though! I'd lose my job…"

"Do you like being a doctor?" asked Dave "You don't seem that into it."

"Gosh no!" said the Doctor. "It's terrible. All those peasants with all their giant boils and plague everywhere. I mean literally EVERYWHERE. You should see Boil Man's backside…"

"Okay, STOP!" said Albrecht. "Could you become a full-time fool?"

"I can't, I just can't!" said the doctor. "I'd lose my leeches! They're the one thing that's made being a doctor bearable."

The doctor really loved his leeches. They did so much together:

Go for long walks in the country.

Have candle-lit dinners.

And stay up late, reading poetry.

"That's a bit weird," said Dave.

The doctor explained that if he quit, the leeches would have to be passed on to the next doctor and that would break his heart.

It's a well-known fact in the medical community that all doctors need leeches.

Peasants in Practice

LEECHES

A CURE FOR EVERYTHING

The Bearded Lady scoffed. "That depends on your methods! I operate a leech-free practice because there are some schools of thought that suggest leeches are icky."

The doctor scowled and hugged his jar of leeches closer. Then he gasped. "Wait, you practice medicine without leeches? So I could keep my leeches?"

"Surely this means we could arrange something

so everyone's happy?" said Dave. "Doctor, are you actually any good at fooling?"

The doctor responded by telling them a terrible joke about shark-infested custard at the same time he tried, but couldn't quite manage, to do a headstand.

"That was terrible," said Albrecht. "But it is probably better than his doctoring. Dave, do you have a plan, and is this going to stop the riot?"

"Yes! Albrecht I'll need your help. Are you much of a performer?"

"*Pfff* are you kidding?!" said Albrecht.

Back at the Dragon's Head the peasants were rioting, despite Gnasty trying to fight them into submission. Just as it was starting to look like Boil Man might burst a boil, there was a loud *GOOOONG!* sound and everyone turned to look at a makeshift stage constructed from boxes. Albrecht leaped into view.

Ladies, gentlemen, and peasants. May I present the one and only DR. HILARITY AND HIS AMAZING PERFORMING LEECHES!

The peasants immediately stopped fighting and started to laugh. Even Gnasty giggled at the shark-infested custard joke. Sharks? In custard? Absurd!

While the crowd was distracted, the Bearded Lady, assisted by Dave, quietly snuck up on any peasant in need of medical attention. Before they had a chance to run off screaming or even glance at her beard, she slapped Band-Aids on wounds and creams on boils, and in some cases just forcefully recommended a good bath.

Afterward, Boil Man came up to Dave, Albrecht, and the Bearded Lady. "Terrific! That man's a much better fool than a doctor. And did you see that leech on the unicycle?... Just amazing! Also that cream the hairy lady gave me has done wonders for my boil. It's shinier than ever now. I'll be going to her with all my ailments. There will be be no more rioting round here."

"AAAAHHH!" A blood-curdling yell cut across the square as Gnasty realized that he'd officially lost the competition and with it, the title of Chief Knight.

He stormed over to Dave and Albrecht. "You interfering little pains in the backside! I'll get you next time, and when I do I'll smash you so hard you'll ..."

But before it could get ugly, he was interrupted by Sir Ironpants sprinting down the street. "The Princess! Something's happened to her! Something terrible. We need all the knights back at the castle. Now!"

RUBELLAS ROOM

KEEP OUT!

CHAPTER 9

Back at the castle, a full Code Pink emergency was underway. Princess Rubella had fallen into a magical slumber and the King had locked himself in her bedchamber and was refusing to let anyone in.

Lip balm?

Outside the bedchamber, an orderly line had formed of knights swigging mouthwash while they waited for the chance to bestow the magical kiss that would wake the Princess.

Dave and Albrecht made their way to the door, but Gnasty, who had been practicing kissing on the back of his hand, spotted them and blocked their way. "Line jumping, eh? I can't have you two getting in the way of me awakening the Princess and getting back in the King's good graces! I'll deal with you once and for all."

Gnasty flung his mouthwash at Albrecht and tried to grab him, but he was stopped in his tracks by a small voice coming through the bedchamber door.

Now this is tasty.

"Dave? Is that my best knight Dave? Let him in at once but the rest of you kiss-mad knuckleheads stay outside!"

Inside the bedchamber, safe from Gnasty, Dave saw that the King was in great distress. "Oh my beautiful Rubella! This is all my fault! I should never have married that terrible woman!"

"Which woman?" asked Dave.

"The Wicked Witch!" said the King, narrowing his eyes. "Ever since the divorce she's been trying to get back at me. She didn't even tell me she was a witch, though I suppose her flying around on brooms and talking to magic mirrors should have been a clue."

"Ah, affairs of the heart are never simple," said Albrecht, sipping his newly-acquired bottle of mouthwash.

I was in love once...

...but she was more woman than I could handle.

Yes, that's all well and good, but I'm trying to explain about Rubella!

"Where was I?" said the King. "Oh yes! The witch always hated Rubella. She was a terrible stepmother, and now she keeps trying to give my Rubella a terrible poison that will cause a hundred years' slumber... USING FRUIT!"

"Not fruit!" said Dave.

"First she tried planting a poisoned apple."

"Then a poisoned orange."

"A poisoned banana."

"Poisoned cherries."

"And even a poisoned watermelon."

"Then that terrible woman changed tactics and left Rubella a poisoned . . . PORK PIE!"

I found poor Rubella curled up asleep covered in pie grease. Now the traditional way to wake her up is with a kiss from a handsome prince, but frankly, none of those bearded idiots outside will do. And just after we'd got past the whole compulsive kissing a frog thing..."

"Is there any other way to break this curse?" asked Dave.

"Well, I suppose the witch could lift it, but there's no way that hag would do it!"

"I could try to talk to her," said Dave. "Do you think you could convince her, Dave?" asked the King. "If you do I'll make you the finest knight that ever lived! With your own castle and . . . and a . . . special hat!"

"A special hat?!" said Dave, "Oh my!"

Oh this thing? That's just my SPECIAL HAT. You know. For being an awesome knight.

107

CHAPTER 10

Dave trotted up to the witch's cottage and knocked on the door. Slowly it creaked open and the witch loomed in the doorway. Dave ducked to

GUTEN TAG!

Hello. Could we have five minutes of your time, please?

avoid a bat and said, "Er, hi. We were hoping to have a quick chat with you about the King?"

"That tiny little idiot!" the witch hissed. "I just knew he'd freak out if I told him I was a witch."

"I can see you're angry," said Dave, "but maybe you'd feel better if you moved on? He's not worth it and you deserve better. Maybe it's time to start dating again?"

The witch explained that she was quite busy these days running a new business designing candy cane conservatories, but admitted dating could be fun.

"*Wunderbar*!" said Albrecht. "I used to be a professional matchmaker so I can set you up on some blind dates."

That night, at the Dragon's Head tavern, emotions were running high.

Date one was not a success.

Date two wasn't much better.

But date three was very, very different.

"Nice work," said the witch. "Ironpants and I are off to the country for a long weekend."

"Wait!" said Dave. "We really need to know how to wake up Princess Rubella."

"Oh fine, I don't even care any more! Just use this." The witch flung something loud and round at Dave as she rode off into the sunset with Ironpants.

Rubella wasn't actually very happy to be woken up and demanded that she have "just five more minutes," but the King was thrilled.

"You are just about the best knight we've ever had, young David! So brave, so clever, so green. I can't believe we had that big oaf Sir Gnasty as Chief Knight," the King chuckled.

Gnasty, who had been listening at the door, turned a deep shade of purple and stormed off.

"Dave!" said the King. "Tonight, I'm going to hold a feast in your honor and there I shall make you Knight of the Special Hat!'

CHAPTER 11

Soon Sir Gnasty had assembled his Army of Evil in the most secluded and secret location in the castle, the downstairs bathroom.

"I call this meeting of the Army of Evil to order!" said Gnasty as he leaned on a toilet.

"Alf?"

"Present!"

"Gary!"

"Present!"

"John?"

"Present!"

"Linda? … Linda!"

"She's just getting the cookies, O Mighty Lord of Evil," said John.

"It is unacceptable to be late to a meeting of the Army of Evil!" raged Gnasty. "What kind of cookies?"

"Butter cookies with jam, I think," said John.

Gnasty considered this. "Good. So, the first item on today's agenda is sharks! Have you acquired the sharks? When the kingdom is mine and I've taken over this castle it's definitely going to need sharks in the moat or it just won't be evil enough."

John looked worried. "Not yet, Sire but Alf was thinking he'd go down to the pet shop tomorrow and ask…"

"UNACCEPTABLE!" roared Gnasty. "Get me sharks immediately, or I'll feed you to them as soon as we have some!"

"Yes ,Your Meanness," said John as he tore off a sheet of toilet paper to mop away the sweat.

"Now, the second item," continued Gnasty. "How's my ingenious plan to kidnap the King going? Soon I shall make him sign the kingdom over to me!"

"Hurrah!" roared everyone, nervously.

"And third. That new wannabe knight Dave has to go! Also, I really want his special hat."

"It is really special, Sir," said Gary.

"SILENCE! It seems this Dave can't do anything wrong. He's always following the instructions in that book, *Knighthood for Beginners*. I'm sure I have a copy somewhere, I'll have to fish it out. He must have a weakness . . . Go and spy on him, my evil army! Bring me any information that could lead to Dave's DOWNFALL! We need him out of the way," said Gnasty, rubbing his hands together in classic villain style.

"Yes, Sir," said the Army of Evil all together.

"Excellent! That concludes today's meeting," said Gnasty. "Now hand me those cookies."

No not for you.

120

At the feast Dave was beside himself with glee. It was a seriously super party with good music, a lot to drink, and rat-on-a-stick for everyone. And, best of all, everybody was being so nice to him.

Dave was thinking he'd really done it. He'd become a brave, clever, and respected knight. Maybe if he kept following the book he could even become the greatest knight of all time? Perhaps minstrels would write songs about him? Or someone would paint a portrait of him riding Albrecht, looking noble? Or... wait a minute, where *was* Albrecht?

Dave spotted him sitting in the corner.
Something wasn't right. Dave went over to see what was wrong and Albrecht hustled him out onto the balcony where they could talk in peace.

"*Meine* Dave, watching you enjoy this disco-teque, strutting about in your special hat has me worried," began Albrecht, looking out into the night. "I have a feeling in my tail that you need to stop worrying about what those metal-headed *dummköpfe* think of you and following their foolish knight rules and start believing in Dave. I did say I would be your life coach, *ja?*"

Dave didn't look convinced. *"I thought your tail was wooden?* And can't you see, Albrecht, the book worked! I used to be a dragon…but now I'm a knight. Dragon…Knight!"

Dave straightened his moustache. "Why would I do things differently if what I'm doing works? And I think I'm pretty good at being a knight now. Look! I've got the special hat and everything!"

Albrecht didn't seem impressed. "I like Dave more when he's being Dave, not a dragon or a knight in a special hat…"

"You're being a big old worry goat. Let's go inside and enjoy the feast."

Sir Dave is a WHAT?!

But they hadn't been alone out on the balcony.

Back inside, Albrecht noticed Linda scurry over to Sir Gnasty, who had been angrily stomping on some canapés. As she whispered something to him Gnasty stopped stomping, grinned widely, and began to stride across the room. Before Albrecht could figure out what was going on, Gnasty had walked right up to Dave.

"Sir Dave!" he began, and Dave turned to look at him a little nervously. "You have truly proved yourself to be a brave, wise, and clever knight having fairly beaten me in all your trials. Now we're all gentlemen here."

Dame Hilda coughed.

"… and ladies of course. We can let bygones be bygones. Why don't I show you where the Chief Knight sits? Up on the top table right next to the King!"

Dave was thrilled. If he'd earned Sir Gnasty's respect, he must be a serious knight. Everyone was clapping as Dave walked up to the top table, but Albrecht pushed his way through the crowd.

"Dave!" said Albrecht breathlessly. "This is very suspicious! When a mean man called Gnasty starts being nice, you have to ask questions..."

"Out of the way greasy goat!" shouted someone in the crowd. Albrecht turned a bit red and looked at Dave expectantly.

"Albrecht, get out the way!" said Dave. "This is a big moment for me and you're being kind of embarrassing."

Albrecht, humiliated, stepped back muttering "... it's not grease ... it's my natural glossiness."

Dave took his seat at the top table between Gnasty and the King. He felt a little starstruck.

The King struggled up onto his chair and began his speech. "Ladies, Gentlemen, Knights, and Princess Rubella, who shouldn't be here because it's way past her bedtime, I welcome you to this feast in honor of Sir Dave! I'm proud to officially award Dave his knighthood for being especially brave, incredibly wise, astonishingly green-skinned and..."

"That's right! He's a princess-eating, gold-stealing dragon!" said Gnasty, triumphantly.

Everyone in the room gasped and started muttering. The King gave a little shriek as Sir Butterball fainted and Princess Rubella started eating all the pork pies while no one was looking.

Dave looked around the room at all the shocked and angry faces and felt himself starting to panic. "I've never done any of those things! Yes, I'm a dragon, but I'm not even a very good one! What I really want to be is a knight, which is why…"

Gnasty started laughing maniacally. "You can't be a knight! You idiot, Dave. Have you even read the final chapter of *Knighthood for Beginners*?"

Dave looked down at the book he was still holding. "No… some of the pages at the back are a bit burned…"

"Well, I think it's time you did," said Gnasty. He pulled out his own copy and showed Dave the final chapter.

HOW TO
SLAY A
DRAGON
CHAPTER 13

Every knight's worst enemy is a dragon. They're dangerous, eat princesses, and their knitting is terrible. It is every good knight's duty to slay them and take their gold.

They hate villages.

They eat all the gold.

They set things on fire.

"Oh my, no!" said Dave. "That dragon looks like Great Aunt Maud!"

People started to scream and panic. Gnasty began chanting, "SLAY THE DRAGON! SLAY THE DRAGON!" and several knights were starting to join in. Dave couldn't believe it. Good, kind, brave knights killing dragons? He felt numb.

The only one not in a panic was Albrecht. He knew he'd have to cause a distraction. Fast.

♩ Aye Aye Aye Aye I like your coconuts!

She really is something.

Finally. I know what it is to love.

Albrecht leaped into action.

While everyone was watching Albrecht, Dave tore his slightly stunned eyes away from the performance and made a quick escape out of the castle.

After a couple of numbers, Albrecht also decided it was time to make a swift exit, even if his fans had other ideas.

Madam! Don't go! You've dropped you shoe! Madam? MADAM! I THINK I LOVE YOU!

As he emerged outside the castle walls, Dave was already working out a plan.

"I know this looks bad Albrecht, but if we can somehow make it look like I've slain a dragon … of course I couldn't actually slay a dragon, most of them are my cousins… but if we make it look like I've slain one then maybe the King will be so impressed with my bravery that he'll get over me being a dragon and…"

"DAVE!" Albrecht cut him off. "That sounds a lot like cheating to me! You are not acting like the Dave I know, you're acting like a *dummkopf* knight, like Gnasty!"

"That's the whole point!" shouted Dave, starting to get angry. "I don't want to be Dave! I want to be a KNIGHT! But how am I going to do that now, eh? How am I going to do anything?! I'm no good at being a dragon and now I can't be a knight."

"Now Dave, when I became separated from the Foreign Legion and was lost in the Mutabu Desert and was forced to eat a cactus…there was one important thing I learned…"

Never have I experienced anything so pointy.

"ENOUGH OF YOUR STUPID STORIES!" yelled Dave. "Everyone knows they're lies! A goat could never do all those things. You're delusional!"

Albrecht looked hurt, but Dave wasn't done.

"You mad old goat, making me do all your crazy schemes and bossing me around all the time. And you know what? You're not even that glossy!"

That was the final straw for Albrecht. "I condition my coat daily as you well know, David! Fine. I can see you don't think you need a trusty steed any more, so you can do it all alone."

"And you do smell goaty," added Dave.

"IT'S A CHARMING MUSK! The saddest thing is Dave, you're a better knight when you're acting like Dave, not following the stupid knight book and trying to be like those *Dummköpfe* back in the castle! Also, I HATE your special hat!"

"How dare you!" said Dave.

"You're a *DUMMKOPF*!" shouted Albrecht.

"No, you're a *DUMMKOPF*!" Dave bawled back.

And they both stormed off in different directions.

Meanwhile back in the castle the King was wandering the corridors with Albrecht's shoe.

"Madam? Madam! I have your shoe! Where are you? Would you like to go for dinner? Let us never be parted! *OOOPH*!" he said as he bumped straight into Sir Gnasty.

"Ah! Gnasty," said the King. "Have you seen the most exquisite lady around here? She has but one single shoe, the hoofiest of feet, and smells kind of goaty."

"*Hmmm*, I think I might have seen her hiding in this huge sack here," said Gnasty ,whipping a sack out from behind his back.

"Excellent. Great job, my good man. At last! My love, we shall be together!" The King toddled into the sack.

CHAPTER 14

Two weeks later …

After taking the King prisoner, Gnasty crowned himself Supreme Evil Overlord and ruled with an iron fist. Everything from brawling to rat-on-a-stick was banned and all cookies were confiscated. In Castletown the peasants became restless and unhappy. This couldn't continue.

Inside the Dragon's Head (recently renamed the Gnasty Arms) the atmosphere was glum.

"Rubella, you're a barmaid now, do you know if there's rat in this pint?" asked the Bearded Lady.

"Who knows?" said Rubella. "Everything's got worse since Gnasty came to power. The drinks, the food. I'm not even sure there's any real rat in the rat-on-a-stick any more, so you'd be lucky if there's some in your drink."

"And whacking injuries are up 200 percent since Gnasty put in place his 'Everyone Will Be Punished With a Whack' policy," added the Bearded Lady. "On the upside my business is doing so well I can finally afford a candy cane conservatory."

"And Albrecht! All he's done since Dave left is sit in the corner and drink mouthwash."

"And what about your father, the King? I hear he's been imprisoned in the dungeons."

"Oh he'll be fine," said Rubella. "He loves slop, especially the XXX Super Hot."

"This isn't right. Something's got to be done."

"Let's form a resistance," whispered Rubella, immediately looking around for spies.

"The peasants' resistance!"

"The peasant and *Princess* resistance."

"Yeah sure. But what we really need is someone who can save the King and take down Gnasty."

Rubella looked concerned. "But all the other knights have gone into hiding because they're far too afraid of him, and even if they weren't, he's stronger than everyone."

"Then we need someone who doesn't need

brute strength. What happened to Dave? He got things done without whacking."

"But Dave is a dragon!"

"Who cares if he's a dragon," said the Bearded Lady. "Everyone thought I couldn't be a doctor just because I'm a bearded lady, so I don't see why Dave can't be a knight just because he's a dragon. Plus, he was a nice guy."

"Good point," said Rubella. "How will we get him back though? I heard he joined a troupe of traveling actors."

"There's only one of us who can convince Dave to come back," said the Bearded Lady, turning to look at the corner of the room.

Rubella raised an eyebrow, but they called Albrecht over anyway. He stumbled over, reeking of peppermint. He wasn't impressed by their plan.

"*Pleh*! I don't associate with the likes of Dave any more. No more *dummköpfe* for Albrecht! I adventure solo now."

The Bearded Lady was having none of it. "Albrecht, even if you're not going to be friends we need him for the sake of the kingdom. Just get him back."

In a field not too far from Castletown, Dave was getting fired.

Dave sighed, took off his costume head and went to sit on a rock away from the other players.

"HULLO!"

"*WAAAHHHH*!" said Dave falling off his rock. "Albrecht! What do you think you're doing here?"

"I've come to take you back, Dave! Gnasty is destroying the kingdom and we need your knight skills to defeat him. But that doesn't mean we're friends! You were very mean about my glossiness."

"Oh, here we go again, always telling me what to do! Anyway, I can't. I don't have what it takes to be a knight, like I didn't have what it takes to be a dragon. Now I'm not even any good at pretending to be a dragon. And I'm definitely not coming back so I can be bossed around by you again."

"The Dave I knew would at least try. I'll get you back to that town or I'll eat my *hintern*!"

So even though Albrecht couldn't convince Dave, they headed back to Castletown anyway.

CHAPTER 15

In the Bearded Lady's consulting room, she immediately started Dave and Albrecht on an intensive session of couples counseling so they could talk about their feelings.

"Dave said some very mean things to me," said Albrecht, folding his arms and looking pouty. "About my coat, my smell, and all my stories!"

"Okay, good progress," said the Bearded Lady, scribbling notes on her pad. "And Dave, what made you unhappy?"

"Albrecht's so bossy! He's always saying we must do this thing because that's how he did it when he was locked in the jungle, or we have to use his GENIUS because it worked when he was in hiding in the frozen North, bah bah bah."

"We're doing some very good work here," said the Bearded Lady. "Dave, I think it might help if you understood each other a little better. Why don't you tell Albrecht about your childhood?"

So Dave explained about the dragon caves, never being a very good dragon, and the summer he spent with Great Aunt Maud the librarian.

"And she gave me a book to take home!" said Dave. "It was called *Fuzzy Bunny's Big Adventure.* You know I was never a very dragony dragon, but somehow when I had this book it was all okay."

"I took it everywhere with me."

"But one day something terrible happened."

"*Mein* Dave?!" said Albrecht "You can breathe FIRE?!"

"Yes, but I don't like to talk about it. It was the

worst day of my life!" said Dave. "I suppose since then I've been looking for another book that'll make everything okay. Also, I really hate butterflies."

"Great!" said the Bearded Lady. "Now Dave, what do you know about Albrecht's past?"

"Loads. He never stops talking about himself."

"But how did a goat come to have all those adventures, Dave? Albrecht, would you like to explain?"

As a child Albrecht was just a normal goat, though perhaps more adventurous than most.

Until one day he was bought by a wizard . . . .

. . . who had plans for him.

The outcome was unusual.

When he had the chance, Albrecht escaped.

But once he got home, things just weren't the same.

So Albrecht set out to see the world, and perhaps even find a place where he'd fit in.

Albrecht had adventures. A LOT of adventures. And he developed a taste for them.

Fisticuffs!

Eventually Albrecht started to feel his age and realized that he'd never really had a chance just to be a goat. So Albrecht retired to a local goat farm to spend some time getting back to his roots.

The problem was he'd forgotten how boring his roots were.

And that's when Dave came along.

"So you see, Dave, it was you who re-ignited Albrecht's sense of adventure with the chance to help you. Maybe he comes across as bossy because he doesn't want you to make mistakes?"

"You had to leave your family too?" asked Dave.

"I don't like to talk about it," said Albrecht.

Dave was shocked by the idea that there was anything Albrecht didn't want to talk about, and he had also started to feel a bit guilty. "I'm sorry Albrecht. I guess I was pretty mean when you were just trying to help."

"Don't worry *mein* Dave," said Albrecht. "When I was trapped on a desert island with only a hamster for company…"

"NO, NO! No stories! Too soon!" Dave stuck his fingers in his ears.

"Okay, okay," said Albrecht. "I'm sorry about my bossiness. It's just because you could be an *über* knight if you…"

"But I can't be a knight. I'm a dragon and if you read the book…"

"You think too much about what the rules are. You saved a princess, *ja*? Stopped peasants from rioting? Won a tournament? But you didn't do it the knight way with whacking and kissing and moustaches. You did it the Dave way, with GENIUS!"

"So," added the Bearded Lady, "is there any reason why you're not a knight?"

"Well, um…" Actually, Dave couldn't think of a reason. So what if he didn't slay a dragon? Slaying things isn't good or kind or wise like a knight should be. Maybe he *was* good at this.

"You…might have a point," said Dave quietly.

"*JA*!" said Albrecht. "You can save the kingdom and do it the Dave way."

"Well, I suppose if there are innocent people in danger I should be brave and try."

"Excellent! I think this has been a very productive session," said the Bearded Lady. "Now GROUP HUG and my bill will be in the post."

You can stop hugging now.

"Right, my trusty steed," said Dave. "Let's go and save the King, and show Gnasty who's really a knight!"

"*Ja!*" said Albrecht. "But first, Dave, I think you're missing something."

Finally, I've got me some new armor.

Hey Ironpants! Want a rematch?

KAW!

CHAPTER 16

Once Dave and Albrecht reached the castle walls they started to think getting in might be a little tricky.

"How are we going to get in there?" asked Dave. "We'd need a whole ARMY!"

"Worry not," said Albrecht. "I have an idea."

"I have sent for help. Now we must wait," said Albrecht.

"O-kaaay. What kind of help?" asked Dave.

"Just some people I know from my travels."

Dave still wasn't sure how true all Albrecht's stories really were, but he didn't want to upset him again. "So, why are seagulls carrying messages for you?"

"I'm their King," said Albrecht. "It's a funny story really…"

"DON'T EVEN START!" said Dave.

Meanwhile, inside the castle things in the throne room weren't going according to plan.

"PEACOCKS?!" yelled Gnasty. "I wanted sharks! All evil hideouts must have sharks! Why did you get these prissy birds?!"

"Um," said Alf. "These were the nearest thing the pet shop had to sharks. Perhaps we could dress them up with fins and…"

"Oooh!" said the King from his little cage suspended from the ceiling. "You must give me the name of that pet shop. I'd like a few more to go in the garden too…"

"SHUT UP! This isn't your castle any more, tiny man! Alan, get him some slop. That always keeps him quiet. Linda, add peacocks to the list of banned things," said Gnasty.

"Oooh, yes! XXX Super Hot Chilli slop for me!" said the King.

Gnasty gave up on the peacocks and lowered himself onto the throne. "Now, Army of Evil! I need you to be on your guard. Things have been too easy for us so far. It's just too quiet. I want everyone on patrol and our defenses tightened. I've got a feeling something's going on…"

The sun had risen high into the sky as Dave sat waiting under the bush. To be honest he was starting to give up hope.

"There's no one coming is there?" he said.

Albrecht peered at his watch. "They should be here soon. I gave the gulls very specific instructions, but sometimes they can get confused or distracted by potato chips."

Then Dave noticed a rumbling coming from the bottom of the ridge. He scrambled out of the bush and peered into the distance. What was that? He thought he saw something . . . wait . . . was that a whale?!

It *was* a whale. A whale being pushed along in a cart by a troupe of straining mud wrestlers. A lot of ballet dancers pranced past them followed by the foreign legion, a tribe of cannibalistic sheep-men, and an old man who could only have been the snakes and ladders master. All people from Albrecht's stories!

On top of that, Dave spied a few familiar faces. Ahead of a group of already-rioting peasants, the Bearded Lady was striding along with a first-aid kit and a club. The other knights had come out of hiding, having obviously been forced there by Rubella, who was prodding them in the right direction with a stick. Even the witch had come along, occasionally blowing kisses at Sir Ironpants as she went. It was a real, if kind of weird, ARMY!

Dave ran up to Albrecht. "I can't believe it! Your stories were all true! You have had a lot of adventures." Dave thought about this and wrinkled his nose. "Really strange adventures. I mean the ballet? Really? Did you really have a fling with the lady whale? And... oh gosh that thing about your tail..." Dave decided not to think about it too hard.

"*Ja*, I did say," said Albrecht. "But we must not get distracted, Dave. This is not the first rebellion I've led, so I shall make a rousing speech to the army and then we'll attack the castle."

"Right, so then I'll sneak in, free the King, and get Gnasty while he's distracted."

"*Über* plan! Now Dave, I've got something for you."

Albrecht rummaged in his pockets and pulled out the book. "I saved it the night of the feast. I thought you might want it now."

Where exactly are your pockets?

Dave looked at the book. "Well, thank you. But… do I need it?"

"I know you'll do the right thing with it. Now there's no time to lose."

Albrecht ran down the hill to greet some old friends, and address his massive, weird army.

He leapt on top of the lady whale and began to shout. *"Guten tag*! I am Albrecht the trustiest of all the steeds! Today we overthrow the Evil Overlord Gnasty! He may whack us, he may take our boils, he may ruin our rat-on-a-stick, but he'll never take our FREEDOM!"

CHARGE!

As the army charged the castle gates, Dave took the opportunity to disappear back into the drains. He was getting to know them rather well by now. After a few wrong turns Dave popped up in the ladies bathroom.

"Oh. Ah. Hello Linda."

After locking Linda in the bathroom (he felt a bit bad about that, but he knew she was a bit of a snitch), Dave snuck through the castle corridors hiding from peacocks and panicking Army of Evil

members who were shouting things like, "We're being attacked by a whale! A WHALE!"

As Dave got closer to the throne room he started to feel his legs go weak and the familiar feeling of needing a bathroom. How was he going to beat a massive knight like Gnasty? If only he'd had a chance to read the single combat bit of the book in more detail… no wait, that's what the old Dave would do. Sir Dave would just go in there, be brave, trust his instincts, and try not to wet himself.

He pushed open the throne room door and peeked inside. Dave let out a sigh of relief when he realized it was empty apart from the King in his cage.

"Ahoy there, David!" said the King. "You're a sight for sore eyes. How's Rubella? Would you like some of this slop? It's the XXX Super Hot."

Dave had an idea. "Stop eating that slop, Sire! You need to throw the bowl at the bars of the cage."

"But it's delicious! One should not waste good slop."

"We can get you more slop later, Your Highness! Do you want to escape or not?"

"Oh yes, escape! How thrilling." The King flung the slop at the bars. With a sizzle and a SLOP, the bars melted away.

The King hopped down and Dave looked curious. "Why were you okay with eating that?!"

"It reminds me of the food we used to have at boarding school," said the King wistfully. "Although we only used to get Classic Brown slop."

That sounds even worse than dragon training, thought Dave. "Hang on a second, Sire, we still have Gnasty to think about."

"*MwahahaHA!* Dave. Oh, I'm so pleased you came back."

Dave spun around.

"Look at you cowering there with your stupid book," said Gnasty with a worrying grin on his face. "Still trying to be a knight are you? Well there'll be no more of your ridiculous dreams because I'm going to squish you so hard the jailer will make slop with what's left."

Gnasty hauled up his mace for the final whack. Dave was more afraid than ever. He did not want to become Premium Dave Slop. Sure that this time he really was going to have an accident, Dave did something without even really thinking. He narrowed his eyes, pulled back his arm, and flung the book at Gnasty.

Gnasty's eyes crossed, and he fell to the floor
with a huge

THWUMP!

CHAPTER 17

HUZZAH! Castletown was celebrating! The King had declared a whole day of feasting in honor of Gnasty's defeat and Dave finally getting his knighthood. The market square was bustling with peasants feasting on rat-on-a-stick, listening to Dr. Hilarity's terrible one-man joke show, occasionally having a little brawl, and being patched up by the Bearded Lady.

Gnasty was wandering about the square with his peacocks. He'd been a changed man since his hit on the head and was a lot easier to be around. He'd also become very fond of the peacocks. Everyone thought he seemed fairly happy, if a bit confused.

A stage had been built in front of the castle. As the bell tolled noon, the King climbed onto the podium followed by Rubella. He scrambled up onto his box and began his speech.

"Ladies, gentlemen, knights, and peasants! This day of celebration is to honor Sir Dave and his bravery in saving both myself and the kingdom. Today I shall officially knight him! First though, I have something important to say. As long as they don't eat anyone's home, set anything on fire, and keep the knitting to a minimum, from this day onward Castletown will be a dragon-friendly town!"

The crowd gave a big cheer, and Dave shot Albrecht a big grin.

"And one last thing. Does anyone know who this shoe belongs to?" The King held up the shoe that Albrecht had dropped when running from the feast.

"Ah there it is!" said Albrecht bouncing up onto the stage and taking the shoe. "I wanted to wear this pair for the ceremony." He put the shoe on.

"You!" said the King "You're my ladylove? But, you're a goat! Well, I swore that I would marry whomever that shoe does fit and, after all, you're still the woman, or goat, I fell in love with. And I admit there is a strange allure about you. Do you still have that pineapple? We can make it work,

can't we?"

"You are so embarrassing," said Rubella, holding her head in her hands.

"Ermm," said Albrecht. "I do not think this is going to work. I'm, er, in a relationship."

Dave raised an eyebrow. That was news to him.

"That's disappointing." The King looked genuinely upset. "Oh well, good luck to you. Anyway, to show my gratitude I have devised the perfect reward. Dave, I would like to offer you Rubella's hand in marriage!"

Dave's mouth dropped open. This could be awkward.

Rubella stepped forward and held up a hand for silence. "No, Father, I love another. I intend to marry my darling Gilbert!" Rubella held up a frog who said, "She loves me for who I am!"

"Oh, right. What? We'll talk about this later young lady!" The King was starting to look quite flustered. "Er, sorry about this Dave. I think just the knighthood will have to do for now."

Dave couldn't have been more relieved.

"Step forward Dave!"

So Dave ascended the stage.

Arise, Sir Dave!

After the ceremony, once the party was in full swing, the other knights were all busy congratulating Sir Dave.

"Good work, old boy!" said Sir Mightybrow, accidentally clapping Sir Ironpants on the back because he'd misplaced his glasses again.

"Now that you're a real knight like the rest of us, you should really think about getting a real steed. I know a used steed dealer who can get you a very glossy one," said Sir Snoz, giving Albrecht a disdainful look.

"Yes!" agreed Sir Butterball spraying pie crumbs all over Dave. "Whoever heard of a knight riding a goat! Haw, haw!"

Dave paused for a moment and then turned to look Albrecht in the eye. "Well I don't remember there ever being a knight who was a dragon, so I see no reason why there shouldn't be a steed who's a goat."

That shut the other knights up.

Dave gave them a little grin and hopped onto Albrecht's back. Albrecht turned and waggled his wooden tail before galloping off into the sunset, where they would have their own party. A better party, with a whale, and bare-knuckle board games, and Albrecht's ex-troupe of ballet dancers pulling out all their moves, and absolutely *no* slop whatsoever.

CHAPTER 18

To make up for Rubella being engaged to a frog, the King gave Dave and Albrecht a fancy house on the edge of Castletown.

Albrecht dropped another box of Dave's books that his parents had sent from the dragons' cave, down onto the kitchen table and looked around contentedly.

"You know I think house sharing will be *wunderbar*!" said Albrecht. "Do you like washing up, *meine* Dave?"

Dave was busy looking through *Knighthood for Beginners*, so he wasn't really listening. Albrecht went over and put an arm around Dave and gave him a squeeze.

"And you did it! You really became a knight. I could not be more proud of you!" He was looking dangerously teary-eyed.

"Yes, I am pleased," said Dave, looking distracted.

"What is it Dave? Are you not happy?" Albrecht asked.

"I am happy," said Dave "but now that it's all over, I think I enjoyed the adventure more than getting the actual knighthood."

"Ahah!" said Albrecht. "You see, this is how it starts, the taste for adventure! You know there can always be more?"

"There can?"

"*Ja*! We could ride off into the sunset now and find another adventure! But you can't ride on my back any more. It aches really badly."

"Have you been using that cream the Bearded Lady gave you? Did you know her real name is Mildred?"

"Yes, of course I have been using the cream. I was supposed to eat it *ja*?"

"You might want to read the label," said Dave. "Funny you should say that about adventure though. I found this page at the very end of the book…"

Want to play?

THIS WAY UP

Albrecht considered the page. "Well, we'd better find a bookshop!"

you might also enjoy...

MY LIFE IN BOILS BY BOIL MAN

FROM THE CREATOR OF RAT-ON-A-STICK

RAT RECIPES

MASTER snakes AND LADDERS BY GAMESMASTER

Accounting for Beginners

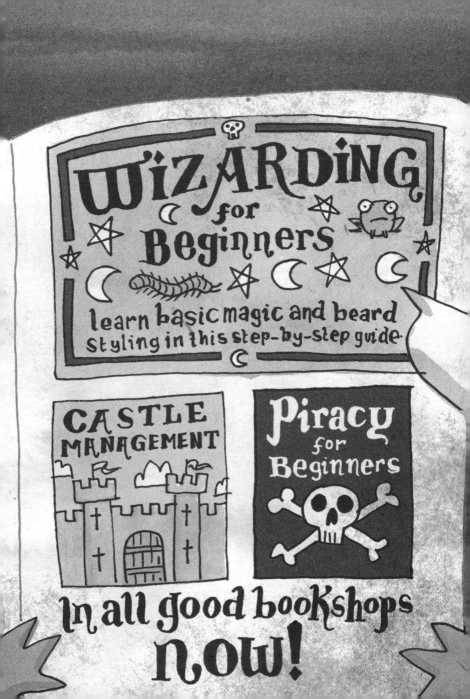

AND THEY ALL LIVED HAPPILY EVER AFTER.

Gnasty became a full-time peacock farmer and never tried to whack anyone ever again.

Rubella went against her father's wishes and married Gilbert the frog. The family was very disappointed when he didn't turn into a prince, but they put in a new pond and had to admit the couple seemed very happy.

Gnasty's Army of Evil disbanded and formed a barbershop quartet. They're now touring the kingdom, but rumor says Linda may go solo due to artistic differences.

The witch and Sir Ironpants broke up but found a shared interest in the construction industry and started the Gingerbread Building Co. together, specializing in candy cane conservatories.

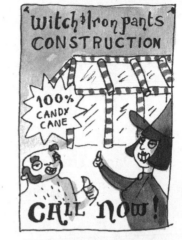

The King never won the heart of his ladylove and to this day still writes terrible poetry about her.

Rat-on-a-stick guy branched out into snake-on-a-stick. It's proving popular despite the occasional poisoning.

Boil Man's boil burst in a freak cart accident. It was a bad day for everyone.

Dame Hilda left the castle and is now pursuing a successful opera career.

Mildred the Bearded Lady is Castletown's most popular doctor ever. She's started a support group for young girls with moustaches.

Dave's parents were very pleased to hear about his success as a knight even though it violates Dragon Lore.

They came to visit Dave and Albrecht, who were both given a lot of new scarfs, mittens, and a lovely hat.

After meeting again at the battle, the Lady Whale and Albrecht decided to give their relationship another try. Albrecht keeps inviting her for dinner, which is challenging because she's much, much bigger than the front door.

Dave and Albrecht have continued to house share, although Dave seems to end up doing all the cleaning, while Albrecht keeps putting his hooves on the furniture. They're sure there'll be more adventures coming their way soon.

Albrecht's German for Dummköpfe

Aufwachen – wake up

Dummkopf – fool, blockhead (singular)

Dummköpfe – fools, blockheads (plural)

Fräulein – Miss, young lady

Guten tag – Good day

Ich kann sprechen – I can speak

Ja – Yes (pronounced Yah)

Kleine – little

Kleiner drache – little dragon

Kleine suppe werfer – small soup thrower

Können sie mich verstehen? – Can you understand me?

Mein – my

Mein dorf esser – my village eater

Meine hintern – my bottom

Meine Gott! Ich kann sprechen! – My God! I can talk!

Mein Dave – my Dave

Mein kleiner grüner (friend) – my little green (friend)

Sauerkraut – pickled cabbage

Schnell – quickly

Über – outstanding, utmost, extremely

Wunderbar – wonderful

Elys is an author and illustrator currently living and working in Cambridge, England. She works predominantly with ink, newfangled digital witchcraft, and colored pencils, of which she is the proud owner of 178 but can never seem to find a sharpener. When not drawing pictures and making things up, Elys enjoys growing cacti, collecting pocket watches, and eating excessive amounts of fondant fancies.

Knighthood for Beginners is Elys Dolan's first young fiction book. Her hilarious picture books have been shortlisted for *The Roald Dahl Funny Prize*, *Waterstones Children's Book Prize*, and nominated for the *Kate Greenaway Medal*.